The Wonderful BOOK

LEONID GORE

The Wonderful Book

SCHOLASTIC PRESS • NEW YORK

LIBRARY OF CONGRESS CATALOGING-IN-PUBLICATION DATA

Gore, Leonid.
The wonderful book / by Leonid Gore. — 1st ed.   p. cm.
Summary: When various forest animals discover a mysterious object in the woods, they each use it
for a different purpose, until a boy reads stories aloud from it, much to the animals' delight.
ISBN: 978-0-545-08598-4 (hardcover)
[1. Books and reading — Fiction. 2. Forest animals — Fiction.]
I. Title. PZ7.G659993Wo 2010   [E] — dc22   2009026348

10 9 8 7 6 5 4 3 2 1   10 11 12 13 14
Printed in Singapore   46
First edition, November 2010

The text type was set in Gill Sans Bold
and Gill Sans Extra Bold.
The display type was set in F 2 F Tagliatelle Bold.
The art was created using watercolor and ink on textured paper.
Art direction and book design by Marijka Kostiw

For

book lovers everywhere,

big and small!

—L.G.

One sunny day,

a rabbit saw something wonderful
while hopping about in the forest.

"What is this?" he asked.

"It will make a cozy little house for me!"

So he wriggled inside,

and there he stayed until . . .

. . . a big growly bear came along!

"Grrrrrrrrrrr!" said the bear.

"That's mine!

It will make a pretty hat for me!"

And he put it on his head and
strutted happily around the forest.

But the bear lost his hat while he
stopped for a snack . . .

. . . and soon a family of mice found it.
"What is this?"
"What is this?"
"What is this?" asked the mice.
"It will make a perfect table for us!"

So they ate their dinner
and scampered away.

At sunset, a tired little fox came along.

"What is this?" asked the tired little fox.

"It will make a comfortable bed for me."

Soon, he fell fast asleep

and had sweet, happy dreams all night long.

The next morning, a hungry little worm
slithered by when he spied
something in the distance.

So he hurried over to take a closer look.

But worms are very slow.

It took him till noon to get there.

"What a tasty-looking flower," said the little worm.

"It will make a delicious lunch for me!"

But just as he was about to take a big bite . . .

. . . along came a curious boy.

"Look at this!" said the boy. "It's a book!

I wonder what it's about!"

So he sat down and began to read.

Soon, everyone gathered around to listen.

They listened as he read about a little rabbit and a big grumpy bear. He read about some hungry mice and a tired little fox.

He read about a little pink worm and
a curious little boy, and much, much more!

"What a wonderful book!" said the boy.

And everybody agreed.